CAPTAIN CAT
AND THE
GREAT PIRATE RACE!

MACMILLAN CHILDREN'S BOOKS

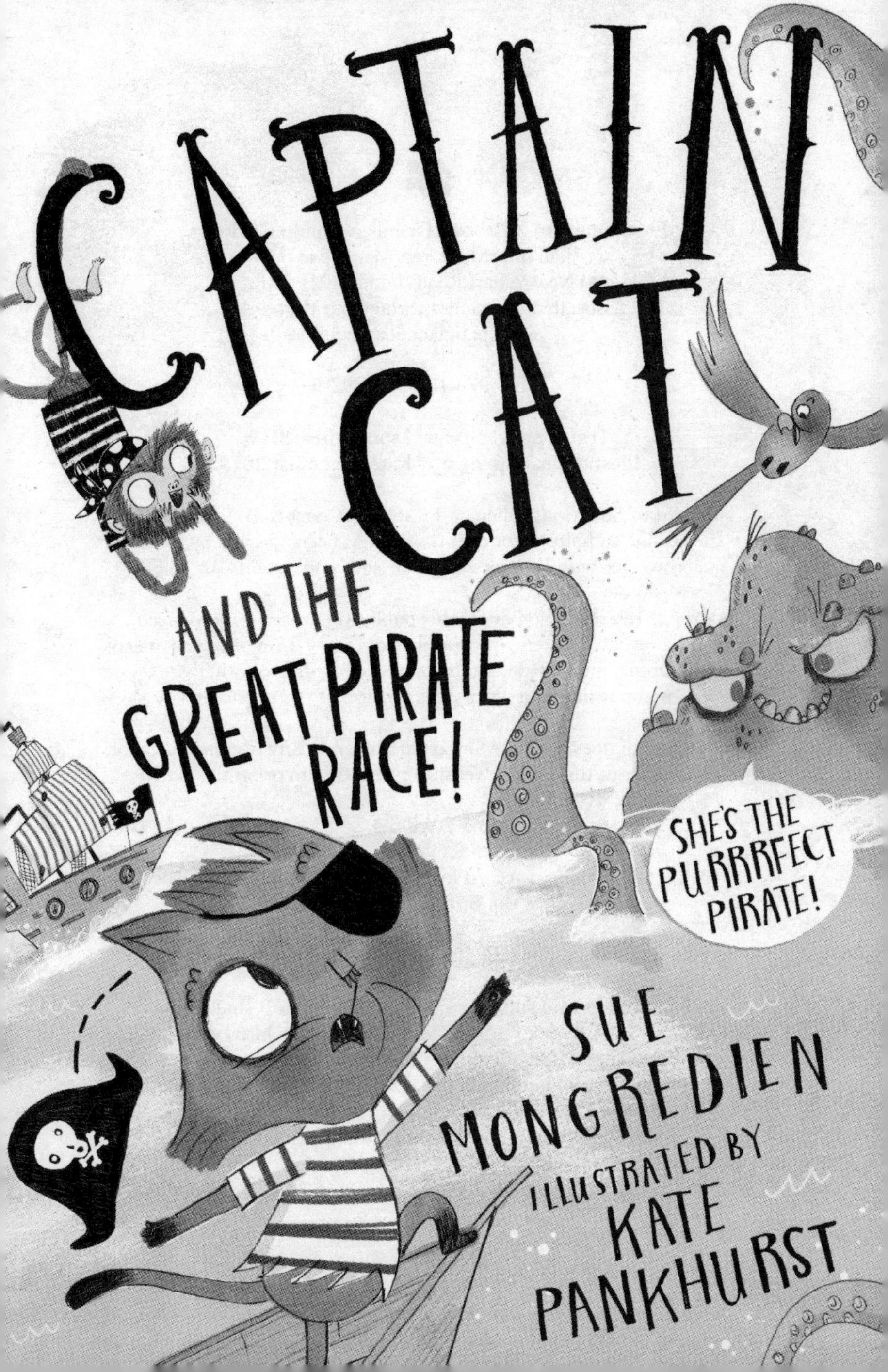

CAPTAIN CAT

AND THE GREAT PIRATE RACE!

SHE'S THE PURRRFECT PIRATE!

SUE MONGREDIEN

ILLUSTRATED BY

KATE PANKHURST

First published 2019 by Macmillan Children's Books
an imprint of Pan Macmillan
20 New Wharf Road, London N1 9RR
Associated companies throughout the world
www.panmacmillan.com

ISBN 978-1-5098-8392-9

Text copyright © Sue Mongredien 2019
Illustrations copyright © Kate Pankhurst 2019

The right of Sue Mongredien and Kate Pankhurst to be identified as
the author and illustrator of this work has been asserted by them
in accordance with the Copyright, Designs and Patents Act 1988.

1 3 5 7 9 8 6 4 2

A CIP catalogue record for this book is available from
the British Library.

Printed and bound by CPI Group (UK) Ltd, Croydon CR0 4YY

This book belongs to:

THE CREW OF THE

PATCH

CUTLASS

CAPTAIN HALIBUT

CANNONBALL

GOLDEN EARRING

MONTY

GINGER

BUTCH

For Colin and Valerie Dailey

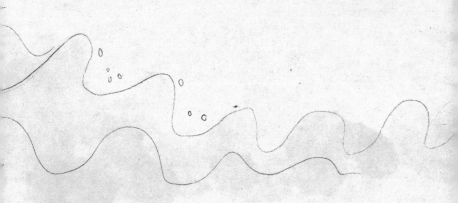

Chapter One

It was a breezy afternoon on board the *Golden Earring* and the crew . . . well, the crew was nowhere to be seen, actually. The pirates had dropped anchor in Ingot Bay earlier that day and were now all enjoying some time on dry land, stretching their sea legs and loading supplies.

Captain Patch the cat was *supposed* to be guarding the ship to make sure they didn't have any unwanted visitors. As the **fiercest** pirate cat on all seven of the high seas, she had a terrifying scowl, a bone-chilling yowl and a growl that would make your hair stand on end.

But don't forget she was also a cat. A cat who really, **REALLY** liked fish. And the smell from the nearby docks was very hard to ignore.

Mmmm . . . fish, she thought to herself, nostrils twitching dreamily at the pong.

It wouldn't hurt to slip away from the ship for a teeny, tiny minute, she decided, watching the fishing boats returning to the harbour with their hauls. You see, as well as being the fiercest pirate cat on all seven of the high seas, Patch also had highly effective tactics when it came to begging for fish.

Sweet little *meow*? Tick.

Friendly rumbling *purr*? Tick.

Cute kitty face? Well . . . she did her best.

Most importantly, she was an expert when it came to winding around a person's legs. If she timed it perfectly, her victim would almost always stumble and trip, sending a nice fat fish plopping down onto the cobbles. **YESSSS!**

How could any cat resist? Patch trotted down the gangplank and got to work. Before long, she was having a whisker-lickingly good time. She polished off some plaice. She had a whole haddock. And she scoffed down some swordfish. *Mmmm!*

Just then, Cutlass, the ship's parrot, landed on a mooring post nearby. 'I say, I say, I say,' he squawked. 'Here's a joke for you, Cap'n! Why did the baby octopus vanish?'

Why did the baby octopus vanish?

Patch picked her teeth with a fishbone and burped gently. 'Did I eat him?' she guessed.

'Nope – he was taken by squidnappers,' Cutlass chuckled. '**Squid**nappers. Geddit, matey?'

'You're squidding me,' Patch groaned. Cutlass might be her best pal, but sometimes his jokes were the *worst*. She gave the fishing boats a last, loving look before she added, 'I suppose we should get back to the *Golden Earring* and guard the ship. This place is full of dodgy-looking pirates.'

He was taken by squidnappers!

'Talking of dodgy pirates,' said Cutlass, 'here comes our crew. And what in Davy Jones's name has Captain Halibut got on his head?'

Patch and Cutlass stared as the *Golden Earring* crew strolled along the seafront together. Talk about a motley bunch.

Leading the way was Captain Halibut, who
had clearly splashed out on a swash buckling
new pirate hat, decorated with very
fancy gold thread.

'Ahoy there, handsome,' Patch heard him say to his own reflection in a shop window.

Next was Cannonball, the ship's cook, who was hauling along a shiny new stew pot. 'Arrrr! This is just what I need for my seaweed casserole recipe,' he said, beaming. 'Special treat!'

Patch and Cutlass both groaned.

'He says "treat", I say "tummy upset",' sighed Cutlass.

Then there was Butch, tucking into an ice cream that was nearly as big as his head. He'd used his last pennies to buy a copy of *The Pirate Comic* too.

'Win your own real treasure map,' he read aloud from the cover as he walked along. 'Nice!'

Patch raised a furry eyebrow at Cutlass. 'Has

he forgotten what happened last time?' she grumbled. After all, when the crew had recently found a different treasure map, there'd been **_explosive_** results!

Finally, there was Ginger, who'd just sent off a new postcard to her mum and dad. She'd also bought some sunglasses, which made her look _extremely_ cool.

There was just one member of the crew missing.

'Where's Monty?' Cutlass asked, looking around.

Monty was the ship's monkey.

'He's at the funfair,' Patch said, pointing towards a huge, rattling rollercoaster that loomed over the sea.

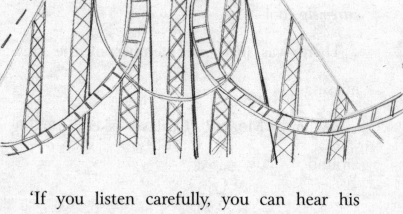

'If you listen carefully, you can hear his screams on the breeze,' she added.

'AAAARRRRGGH^{H}H^{H}HH!

W H O O A A A A A A A A ! '
they heard just then.

' E E E E E E E E !

W O O - H O O - H O O O O O ! '

Patch and Cutlass grinned at one another . . . but the smiles were wiped off their faces the very next second when they heard a sneering voice.

'**ARRRR!** Wallowing walruses, if it isn't Captain Halibut himself!'

Patch's fur prickled immediately. Her tail puffed up like a bottlebrush.

Cutlass's feathers trembled. 'Is that . . . ?' he asked.

'Yep,' replied Patch as they turned and eyed the tall pirate walking towards the *Golden Earring* crew. It was Captain Crunchbone, a **vile** villain and Halibut's sworn enemy. He had a bushy red beard, a gold front tooth and a bone through his nostrils. 'What's *he* doing in Ingot Bay, I wonder?'

12

Being far too
stupid to know
animal
languages,
the pirates
only heard
a meow and
couldn't understand
what Patch was saying.

But the *Golden Earring*
crew had noticed Crunchbone too.

Butch gave a nervous whimper. '*Eep!*'

Ginger peered anxiously over her new

sunglasses. 'Uh-oh.'

Cannonball whipped a rolling pin out of his

apron pocket and brandished it. 'Grrr!'

Then there was a cross-sounding **CLONK** as Captain Halibut stamped his wooden leg. 'Crunchbone, you horrible hagfish,' he said coldly. 'We meet again.' He tilted his snazzy new hat so that the sunshine twinkled brightly from the gold stitching, but if Crunchbone was impressed he didn't show it in the slightest.

'Halibut, you poxy poltroon,' replied Crunchbone, curling his lip. 'And there was me hoping you might have drowned by now, and be just a heap of old bones at the bottom of the ocean.' He laughed meanly, showing blackened teeth. 'No such luck!'

'Ouch,' said Patch to Cutlass. 'Now that's harsh.'

Captain Halibut glared his most **fearsome** glare at Crunchbone. 'If you've quite finished your **gibbering**,' he growled, 'I've got a ship to sail.'

'The *Golden Toilet*? Arrrr! Next you'll be telling me you're entering the Great Pirate Race with her tomorrow,' Crunchbone snorted. '**Ha ha ha ha!**'

Captain Halibut's eyes blazed. He didn't take kindly to anyone insulting the *Golden Earring*, least of all his old enemy. 'How dare you?' he thundered. 'At least I've *got* a ship. As I recall, last time I saw you and your mangy crew, your rotten boat was on *fire*!'

Crunchbone gave a scornful laugh. 'That old thing,' he sneered. 'Have you not seen what

I'm captain of these days?' He pointed at the dock. 'Made an insurance claim, didn't I? Take a look at the *Dastardly Plunderer* over there, me hearties. She's mine, all mine.'

Everyone turned to follow Crunchbone's finger.

'**Wowzers**,' gulped Patch as she saw where he was pointing. The *Dastardly Plunderer* was a **huge** and handsome ship indeed, with a **massive** skull-and-crossbones flag, impressive shiny cannons and not one, not two, but **THREE** lookout points. Plus the mast looked *really* good for claw-sharpening.

'Cor,' sighed Ginger longingly. 'What a beauty.'

'Imagine the kitchen on that,' murmured

Cannonball with a dreamy expression.

'I bet the crew cabins have proper beds and everything,' said Butch, whose bunk was so tiny that he had to sleep with his feet sticking out at the end every night.

As for Captain Halibut, he just made a choking sound, too jealous to even speak.

Patch glanced back over at the *Golden Earring* with its tatty sails, its tangled rigging and shabby cabins, and felt a tingle of envy herself. Next to the *Dastardly Plunderer*, it looked a complete wreck.

Captain Crunchbone smirked a horrible gloaty smirk. 'Good, eh? I reckon there'll only be one winner of the Great Pirate Race tomorrow,' he said. 'And something tells me it won't be *you*, old Halibobs.'

Patch had never heard of the Great Pirate Race and she was pretty sure Captain Halibut hadn't either – which was why she was surprised when he snapped, 'Oh, *really?* We'll just see about that. Fifty gold coins says *we'll* win it, thank you very much! **Arrrr!**'

Captain Crunchbone hooted with laughter and slapped his raggedy-trousered thigh. 'Ha ha! In your dreams, sunshine.'

Meanwhile, the rest of the *Golden Earring* crew were gazing at one another in alarm.

'Great Pirate Race?' whispered Ginger. 'Do you have to be great to enter it, do you think, or can any old pirate take part?'

Butch's enormous knees were knocking together. 'I don't like the sound of it,' he muttered anxiously. 'I've got a bad feeling about this race. It might be **dangerous**!'

'I'd better stock up on grub,' Cannonball fretted. 'Maybe some jellyfish fritters will help the captain run faster.'

'Run faster?' repeated Captain Crunchbone, overhearing. He threw back his head and laughed so hard that the bone through his nostrils  waggled. *'Run faster?* Bellowing barnacles, Halibut, you've got a crew of dimwits here and no mistake! The Great Pirate Race is a *sailing* race, not a running race – from Ingot Bay to Hammerhead Island. Ha! I'll see you at the finish line . . . when you arrive there in last place. As long as your crummy old ship doesn't sink on the way!'

And, with that, he barged past Halibut, still

sniggering, and disappeared into the Piratical Emporium of Bloodthirsty Bargains.

'That flame-haired **flounder**,' growled Captain Halibut. 'That rotten-toothed **rogue**. He'll be laughing on the other side of his ugly face when we romp over the finish line in first place and seize the prize. Just you wait!'

Chapter Two

'Seize the *prize*?' Patch repeated to Cutlass. 'Since when has our crew ever won a prize for anything in their lives?'

'Most Hopeless Bunch of Pirates?' suggested Cutlass, scratching his head with a claw.

'That's possible,' Patch agreed. 'But come on – a sailing race? They've got no chance!' She glanced over to see that the *Golden Earring* crew was now huddled around a map, talking in low voices. 'Oh no,' she groaned. 'I think they're actually taking it seriously. Look at

Halibut's face! He means business.'

'We can do this, me hearties,' Halibut was saying, jabbing so hard at the map that he nearly stabbed his finger through it. 'Even if it kills us!'

'Um . . .' said Ginger, who could see a teeny-weeny problem with this outcome.

'I don't want to be *killed*,' whimpered Butch, his lower lip wobbling.

'Why don't we go and have a nice cup of tea instead, Cap'n?' Cannonball suggested. 'Perhaps a tasty ship's biscuit too. Crunchbone's just a big show off. We should ignore the silly sausage.'

'*Tea? Biscuits? Silly sausages?*' roared Captain Halibut in disgust. 'Call yourselves *pirates*? Yo-ho-ho, and a bottle of rum – that's what we need. Not to mention a devilishly good plan for winning this rascally race. Follow me!'

And off he stamped, wooden leg clonking, towards the Scurvy Scoundrel Rum Parlour, with the rest of the worried-looking crew trailing behind.

Patch licked a paw, thinking hard. 'How can we help our pirates?' she said. 'Or at least stop Crunchbone from winning the Great Pirate Race?'

Before Cutlass could answer, they saw a familiar figure staggering towards them: Monty, who had sneaked on to all the scariest rollercoasters at the funfair and whose legs were now as wobbly as jelly.

'**AMAZING!**' he yelled when he saw them. 'That was **AMAZING!**'

'Monty! Just in time,' Patch cried. 'We need your help.'

'*Ooh.*' Monty stopped and put his hand to his tummy. '*Ooer.* I feel a bit . . . I feel a bit sick.'

'Aim for the *Plunderer*!' Cutlass squawked with a chuckle.

He was only joking, but his words gave Patch an idea.

'Yes!' she cried. 'Guys, if Captain Crunchbone thinks we're going to let him win this pirate race, he can think again. Come on! Let's check out his fancy new ship. Maybe we can leave him a few nasty surprises . . .'

She scurried up the gangplank of the *Dastardly Plunderer*, while Cutlass flew overhead. Monty limped behind, still clutching his belly.

'What are we doing here?' he groaned, stepping on to the deck. But before anyone could reply . . .

BLEEEEUUUGGH! He was sick *everywhere*.

'Oh dear,' Patch said, trying not to laugh. 'Let's hope our dear friend Crunchbone doesn't accidentally step in that!'

'I really hope nothing
else happens to this
lovely new ship,' Cutlass
said naughtily, before he

flapped over to the ship's wheel and
plopped parrot poo on
the handles.

Giggling, Patch
and her pals set about
making their mark on
the *Plunderer*.

Patch coughed up a furball
on Crunchbone's pillow.
Cutlass pecked at the
captain's alarm clock

to change the settings, so that an alarm would go off at midnight. And, once Monty had finished being sick, he set about tangling the rigging ropes into a complete monkey puzzle.

'That'll teach Crunchbone to be rude about our ship,' Patch declared with a triumphant tail-twitch before they hurried away once more.

Over on the *Golden Earring*, Captain Halibut had gathered the crew together in the map room.

'Good news, me hearties! I have come up with a dastardly dirty plan,' he smirked, just as Patch, Cutlass and Monty sneaked back in.

'Arrrr!'

He unrolled a map
on the table and
held the corners
down with two
bottles of rum,
a compass and a
framed picture of
his mother, the
terrifying Gloria
Blunderbuss.
Everybody leaned
in closer to look.

'So, see here,
the course of the
race is marked

The Sea lot REALLY REALLY, BAD Things

RUM

START

FINISH

in red,' Halibut went on, pointing out the long, rambling route. 'But I propose that we cunning old seadogs take *this* sneaky shortcut to Hammerhead Island instead. Right through the **Sea of Really, Really Bad Things**.' He dragged his finger straight from Ingot Bay to the finish line, leaving a greasy mark on the map. 'Ha ha!'

Ginger frowned. 'But . . . wouldn't that be . . . cheating?' she asked.

'**Pah!** Who cares about that?' scoffed the captain.

Butch had turned pale. 'I don't like the sound of the **Sea of Really, Really Bad Things**,' he said, his voice trembling. 'It sounds really, really . . .' He shrugged. 'I can't think of the word, but not good.'

'Bad?' suggested Cannonball.

'Yes! Bad! It sounds really, really bad,' replied Butch, teeth chattering.

'**Pish! Bosh! Codswallop!** It's just a silly name,' the captain scoffed. 'It doesn't *mean* anything. Anyway, do we want to win this blasted race, or what? Yes!'

There was a moment's silence where the other pirates looked at one another. 'Well . . .' began Cannonball nervously, scratching his neck with a spatula.

'You know, there are some *other* cool pirate competitions we could enter instead,' Ginger put in, pulling a crumpled leaflet from her back pocket. 'Let's see . . . Best-dressed Pirates.

Bravest Pirates. Scariest Pirates . . .'

'Stupidest Pirates . . .' Patch murmured to Cutlass.

But Captain Halibut only had one competition on his mind. 'As I was saying, we DO want to win the Great Pirate Race,' he declared. 'And this is how we're going to do it . . .'

As the pirates plotted their course, Patch heard a faint scratching sound behind her. She spun round immediately, but nothing was there . . . apart from a strange smell. *A strange animal smell,* she decided, sniffing hard and frowning. That was odd. Where was it coming from?

Nose to the floor, she left the map room,

trying to follow the scent. But as she padded

along she had the strangest feeling

that she was being watched.

She turned left. Nobody there. She turned

right. Nobody there. She turned in a complete

circle. Nobody there.

Patrolling the poop deck to make sure all

was shipshape, her ears pricked up as she heard

what sounded like whispery voices. A scrabble of claws. *It must be the wind in the rigging*, she decided after a moment. *Maybe even Monty playing one of his silly tricks. Right?*

Patch continued around the ship, checking everything carefully. The cannons were gleaming, the ropes neatly coiled, the gunpowder barrels carefully stacked. The pirate flag flew proudly from the mast while strings of clean laundry flapped overhead. Everything looked perfectly normal, in other words. So why did she feel so uneasy?

Just then, she rounded the edge of the gun deck and saw . . .

'**RATS!**' she cried, as two of the little stinkers scuttled past her. She charged after them at once, thundering down the deck at top speed. 'Not so fast, you **rotten rodents**!' Her mind racing as fast as her feet, she realized with a groan that the rats must have scurried up the gangplank and stowed away earlier that day. While *she* was meant to be guarding the ship! But how many of them were now on board the *Golden Earring*?

'Prepare to be pounced on!' she yowled, fur bristling as she pelted after them.

'Cat alert! Quick!' the rats squeaked as they sprinted ahead. Unluckily for Patch, there was a third rat up in the rigging, who saw what was happening . . . and with one quick chomp of his yellow ratty teeth, he bit right through the washing line above her.

SNAP! went the washing line, breaking and collapsing.

FLUMP! went the wet clothes, landing on the deck in damp clumps.

'Waahhh!' wailed Patch, as a pair of Cannonball's big saggy pants dropped right on her head. Although her ears were covered, she could just make out the sound of squeaky ratty giggles, as well as Monty, helpless with laughter.

'Ha ha ha ha ha ha!' he chortled, clutching at his sides.

Struggling out from under the wet washing, Patch growled crossly. *Wretched rats!* How dare they board her ship? Did they not recognize a pirate cat when they saw one?

'I thought cats were meant to be good

hunters? Not much of a ratter, are you?' Monty

cackled, almost falling off the rigging in his

glee.

'All right, all right,' Patch muttered, twitching

her whiskers. She knew Monty was only teasing,

but she couldn't help feeling embarrassed all the same. As the ship's cat, catching rats was her job. And it was her fault that they were on board the *Golden Earring* in the first place!

What's a rat's favourite game?

'Reminds me of a joke,' squawked Cutlass, flying over just then. 'I say, I say, I say: what's a rat's favourite game?'

Hide and squeak!

'I don't know,' sighed Patch, stepping away from the soggy laundry.

'Hide and squeak!' laughed Cutlass. 'Geddit, matey? Hide and *squeak*!'

Patch managed a small smile. 'Good one,' she said, then squared her furry shoulders. 'Well, the rats may be hiding, but I'm going to have to find them. Because if Captain Halibut discovers that I've allowed them on board his ship . . . I'm in deep trouble!'

Chapter Three

The following morning, the ship's gong went **CLANG!** at a horribly early hour as the captain set about waking everyone up. '**Ahoy! Rise and shine!**' he bellowed. 'Today's the day we win the Great Pirate Race. Look lively! Shake a leg! Put your best winning pants on.'

'Um . . .' said Butch. 'I've only got one pair of pants. So . . .'

'Want to borrow some of mine?' asked Cannonball. 'I've got some nice Brussels sprouts-patterned ones . . . Or these ones have a cool cabbage design . . .'

Cutlass cackled, overhearing this. 'Next he'll be offering some with a pea print. *Pee print,* geddit?'

'Stop,' yawned Patch, putting her paws to her ears. 'It's too early to think about jokes. Or pants, for that matter.' Patch was extremely tired. She'd been up all night trying to catch the rats, but hadn't managed to nab a single one. *They must have found themselves a* really *good hiding place,* she thought wearily. *But where?*

Cutlass noticed her glum face. 'Hey, don't worry, Cap'n Cat,' he squawked. 'You know how stupid our crew is. They'll be so busy today with this pirate race that they won't even notice any extra ratty passengers on board.'

But just then there came a thunderous shout from Captain Halibut's quarters. **'What the devil?'** he roared. 'I've just chased a revolting rodent out of my cabin. And look what it's done to my new *hat*!'

Patch's whiskers wilted immediately. 'Uh-oh,' she said, slinking away in the opposite direction.

Then, as she passed the kitchen, there came a furious yell from Cannonball. **'Who's been nibbling my bread rolls?'** he bellowed, followed by the sound of crashing saucepans. 'Go on, get out of it! Shoo!'

'Oh dear,' sighed Patch, ducking as a frying pan came flying through the door.

45

She hurried past the map room just in time to hear a wail of woe.

'**Disaster! DOOM!**' cried Butch. 'Don't panic, everyone, but something has chewed great big holes in our map, and it wasn't even me. Now we won't know how to get to Hammerhead Island!'

'This is not good,' groaned Patch, her tail sagging in dismay.

She slunk past the cabins, only to hear Ginger's cross shout next. '**Hey!** Who's eaten all my emergency snacks?'

Patch was pretty sure she knew who'd eaten Ginger's emergency snacks. She could guess who might have chewed through the map, nibbled the bread rolls and wrecked Captain

Halibut's new hat too. It sounded as if the rats had been causing trouble all over the place behind her back!

Captain Halibut *stamp*-clonked on to the deck in a terrible temper. His face was purple with rage and his hat was missing half its brim. **'Devil's dogfish!** This is a bad business,' he growled.

Butch rushed over with the ruined map. 'Captain, look!' he cried. 'I'm not one to panic, but I don't think we should even *start* the race now that we don't know where to go. Why don't we have a nice day at the seaside instead? Paddle in the sea, snooze in deckchairs and—'

The captain looked as if he might explode at this lily-livered suggestion. 'Seaside? Deckchairs?

Call yourself a bloodthirsty pirate?' he snapped. 'We're taking part in that race, man, and we're going to win. Do you hear me? We're going to *win*!' Just at that moment, he spotted Patch, trying to slink out of sight, and his eyes went very narrow and squinty. 'And if we *don't* win we'll know who to blame: that useless, good-for-nothing, scraggy old mog for letting the ship become overrun with rats!' He shook his fist at Patch and snarled, his gold tooth glinting in the morning sun. 'I'm warning you here and now, fleabag. Get rid of those rodents, and fast . . . otherwise you'll be **walking the plank**!'

Head down, Patch scuttled off to find her friends, feeling very sorry for herself. 'What am I going to do?' she cried. 'You heard

Captain Halibut: if I don't catch the rats, I'll be overboard – nine lives and all!'

There came a squeaky, sneaky snigger from behind them and Patch whirled round at once – but the deck seemed empty. Where *were* those rats?

'You couldn't catch a *cold*, Patch, let alone every rat on this ship,' scoffed Monty, shaking his head. 'Your days are numbered. The big question is . . . Once you've walked the plank, do I swap to your bed or keep my own?'

'Hey!' cried Patch, swiping a paw at him.

'Aw, mate,' said Cutlass kindly. 'Don't worry. You're a cat – and you moggies always land on your feet. Right?'

'Apart from when we're being dropped into the depths of the ocean,' Patch replied gloomily. If only she had paid better attention to the ship while they were in Ingot Bay, they wouldn't have this problem! Why had she let herself be tempted by the fish?

50

Snigger. Snort. Snuffle.

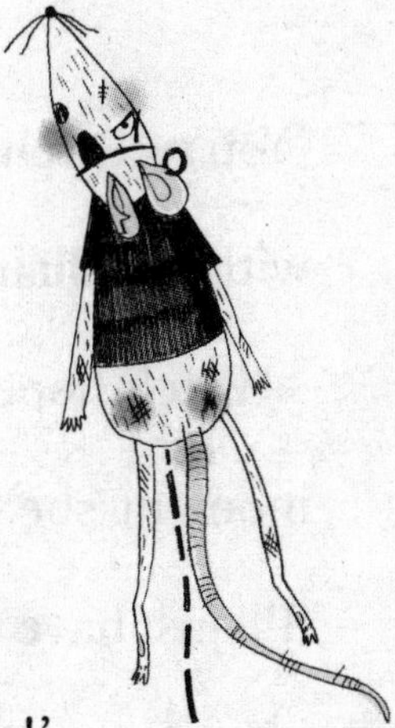

'Hope you're a good swimmer!'

tittered a squeaky, ratty voice.

'Hope you're *not* a good

swimmer!' giggled another one.

'Be quiet, you rascally wretches!'

growled Patch. 'Or I'll—'

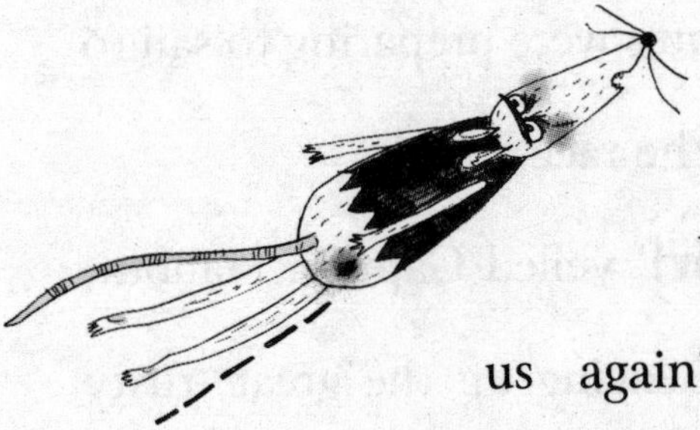

'Or you'll

what? Not

be able to catch

us again?'

sniggered a third

ratty voice, followed by gales

of high-pitched squeaky laughter.

'Hee hee hee!'

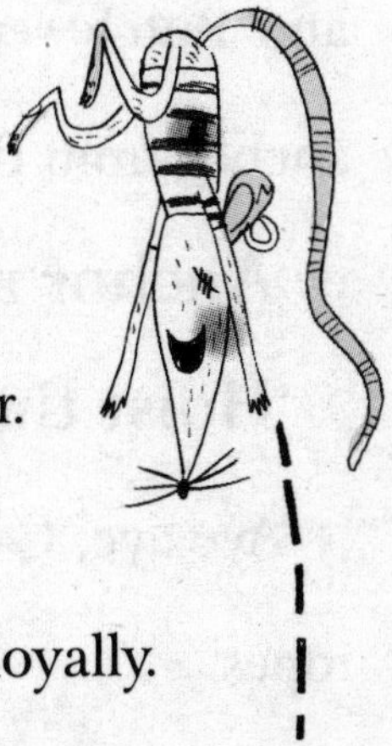

'Ignore them,' Cutlass said loyally.

'You're Patch, our Captain Cat! You'll come up with a brilliant plan soon. I know it!'

Patch hoped her friend was right, but at that moment she did not feel confident *or* brilliant. 'I'll just have to keep searching,' she said, setting off to prowl around the ship once more.

Meanwhile, the pirates were preparing to sail to the starting line of the race.

'**Weigh anchor!**' yelled Captain Halibut, and Butch set to, heaving up the great, rusty anchor from the seabed.

'**Anchor away!**' he called back.

'**Hoist the sail!**' ordered Captain Halibut.

'Aye aye, Cap'n!' cried Ginger, hauling at the ropes.

The *Golden Earring* set off and soon reached the start of the Great Pirate Race on the other side of the harbour. There was a huge buzz of excitement in the air. A band played on the dockside. Bunting flapped. Crowds of people were cheering and waving banners. Even the town mayor was there with a special silver whistle hanging round his neck.

'Welcome, everyone, to the annual Great Pirate Race,' he boomed through a megaphone.

'The first crew to reach Hammerhead Island will be the winners. Good luck to all you pirates taking part. On your marks, get set . . . **PEEEEEP!**' He blew into the whistle and the competing ships began to sail away. 'Yay! I love races,' Ginger cried excitedly from up in the crow's nest, waving to the other crews. Not everyone was quite so friendly, though. In fact, some of the pirates were positively **mean**.

'Arrrr!' yelled a pirate from a ship called the *Howling Curse*, throwing rotten vegetables at the rival ships.

'Mmmm, I'll use that for tonight's dinner,' said Cannonball, licking his lips as a mouldy cabbage plopped on to the gun deck and a surprised-looking snail tumbled out.

'Fire in the hole!' bellowed a pirate from the *Mighty Man-O'-War*, before blasting a cannon at a ship called the *Savage Wolf*.

As for Captain Crunchbone, he was taking the whole race *very* seriously: barking orders to his crew, scowling into the distance and occasionally shooting his blunderbuss into the air for effect. **BOOM! BOOM!**

'Pah!' scoffed Captain Halibut. 'He's all bluff and bluster. Besides, only one pirate in this race has the brains to win!' He winked at his crew. 'We'll hang back, me hearties. Let the others work up a sweat. Then we'll swerve off on our shortcut while nobody's watching. Arrrr!'

On they sailed through the choppy waters, soon falling behind the other ships. Although Captain Halibut seemed full of confidence in his plot, nobody else on board the *Golden Earring* seemed in a very good mood.

Down in the kitchen, Cannonball had accidentally set fire to his favourite apron while wearing it and was now beating himself with saucepan lids,  trying to put out the flames.

'Aaargh! Ooh! Ow!' he yelped.

Up in the crow's nest, Ginger shouted in dismay as the wind snatched her brand-new sunglasses off her head and blew them far out to sea. **'Noooooo!'**

And over on deck, Butch was getting his knickers in a total twist about where they were headed.

'Don't panic,' Patch heard him say to Captain Halibut as they stood together at the ship's wheel, 'but we're miles behind all the other pirates and we don't even know where this shortcut *is* now that the map is ruined.' His bottom lip began to tremble and his voice became high and wobbly. 'What if we never find our way back home again?' Tears welled in his eyes. 'What if we've already sailed right into the Sea of Really, Really Bad Things? We're **DOOMED!**' he wailed.

'Piffling pilchards, what nonsense!' Captain

Halibut snapped in reply. 'Are we pirates or are we great big babies? We don't need maps to tell us where to go. We can use our seafaring brains to have our own adventure.' He stamped his wooden leg with a loud *thunk*. 'Besides, I've told you a hundred times, the Sea of Really, Really Bad Things is only a silly name. It's probably not even a real place. Let's just keep going and—'

'Ahoy!' called Ginger from up in the lookout. 'There's some kind of *sign* ahead, mateys.'

'A sign!' echoed Butch, brightening. He gazed out at the horizon. 'Captain, what does it say?'

Captain Halibut peered through the telescope. 'It says . . . Welcome to the Sea of . . .' Then he broke off, looking flustered, and put

the telescope behind his back. 'Er . . . nothing,'
he said.

'The Sea of Nothing?' Butch repeated,
scratching his head. 'Sounds a bit boring.'

'The sign says', Ginger yelled, holding up
a pair of binoculars, '"Welcome to the Sea of
Really, Really Bad Things." Ooh, gosh. So it *does*
exist. And we're in it!'

welcome to the
SEA OF
REALLY, REALLY
BAD THINGS
sail safely!

'**HELP!**' screamed Butch, clapping his hands to his face and quivering like a jellyfish. 'We need to turn back! The Sea of Really, Really Bad Things will be full of **really, really bad things**. Like dangerous sharks and sea monsters and icebergs and . . .'

'Lunch in ten minutes!' came a shout from Cannonball just then. 'Eel stew, good and gooey. I hope you're hungry, me hearties!'

'. . . And **EEL STEW!**' Butch groaned, shuddering. He sank to his knees dramatically.

'The bad things have already started!'

'Blow me down.' Captain Halibut frowned as a **horrendous stink** came wafting up from Cannonball's kitchen. 'You've got a point there, matey,' he admitted, eyes watering.

Patch and Cutlass caught a whiff of the stew as well.

'*Poo,*' said Patch, fanning a paw in front of her face. 'Do you think that stew is going to taste as bad as it smells?'

'Don't be *stew-pid*, Cap'n,' Cutlass joked. 'It's going to taste a lot worse than that.'

Meanwhile, Captain Halibut seemed to be having second thoughts about his shortcut.

'Look, I'll tell you what we'll do,' he said to Butch. 'We'll drop anchor at the first island we get to, pick up a new map and then plot a different course, away from the Sea of Really, Really Bad Things. Okay? Although we can't dilly-dally. We still want to win this here Great Pirate Race. Arrrr!'

'**LAND AHOY!**' called Ginger just then from up in the crow's nest.

'There!' Captain Halibut beamed. 'That didn't take long. Prepare to drop anchor, me hearties. **Heave ho!**'

'**Land ho!**' Butch cheered, steering towards the green island that loomed ahead.

'I might even be able to buy a new hat there,'

the captain said happily. 'We'll have plenty of time, seeing as we're going to win this race so easily.'

Hearing a rustling sound behind her, Patch turned just in time to see a scaly rat tail vanishing down the stairs, too fast for her to catch.
She hissed in annoyance. 'Let's hope our rats decide to scuttle off the *Golden Earring* and on to this island,' she said to Cutlass. 'Paws crossed!'

Little did Patch know, however, that they were about to come face to face with a whole new problem.
A monstrous problem! Because, as the pirate crew steered towards the green island, they were all surprised to see its hills give a sudden ripple.

The entire island seemed to shake.

'What's going on? Is there a volcano?' Patch wondered, staring in confusion. 'An earthquake?'

'That's no island!' Butch yelped as they sailed round the side of it and had a better view. Then he let out a shrill shriek. 'Nobody panic but . . .

IT'S A SEA MONSTER!'

Chapter Four

Chaos broke out at once on the *Golden Earring*. Butch collapsed on the deck, whimpering and wailing.

Monty raced up the rigging to the crow's nest, where he leaped into Ginger's arms.

Patch's fur tingled all over as she took in the enormous size of the sea monster that lay snoozing in the water ahead. It was absolutely

HUGE.

GIGANTIC!

Maybe Butch had been right to fear the Sea of Really, Really Bad Things. A monster like that could chomp them all up in a single gulp!

'Pipe down, you *blithering blowfish*!' hissed Captain Halibut, poking Butch with his wooden leg. 'Pull yourself together, man! Yes, that *is* a sea monster . . . but it seems to be asleep. Bring the ship about, crew, and let's get out of here *fast*. And don't make a sound, whatever you do. The last thing we want is to wake the beastie up.'

'Aye aye, Cap'n,' whispered Ginger, patting Monty's head kindly before scrambling down the rigging to help the others. Butch took a deep breath and tiptoed across the deck to the wheel, heaving it starboard to haul the ship round. If Patch hadn't been so scared of the sea monster herself, it would have been quite funny to see the pirates sneaking about, whispering in teeny, tiny voices as they steered the *Golden Earring* away. Even the captain managed not to *stamp*-clonk his way around for once.

69

But all of this quiet, careful calm couldn't last for long. Just as Ginger was edging delicately backwards across the deck, Cannonball came round the corner, carrying a massive pan of hot, foul-smelling stew.

'Grub's up!' he yelled, making everyone jump.

'Whoa!' cried Ginger, colliding with him.

CRASH! went the pan as Cannonball dropped it on the deck.

SPLAT! went the eel stew as it splashed against Ginger's bare legs.

'Ouch! Ow! **YeeeoooWW!**' shrieked Ginger, scalded by the hot liquid.

Captain Halibut turned purple with rage. 'Be **QUIET!**' he yelled furiously. 'Remember, we've got to **BE QUIET!** Otherwise—'

'Um . . . Captain,' Butch gulped just then.

Patch's tail puffed up with fright as she saw the sea monster twitch at all the noise. Oh no. Was it waking up?

'Otherwise we'll disturb that hideous old brute of a monster and—'

'**CAPTAIN!**' Butch hissed in his loudest, most urgent whisper.

Patch froze on the spot as the sea monster opened one large and terrible red eye, as big and round as a dustbin lid.

'And I bet it looks even uglier and more disgusting when it's awake, so—'

'*CAPTAIN!*' Butch hissed again. '**BE! QUIET!**'

The sea monster let out a blood-curdling roar, so terrifying that the captain's mouth swung shut with an abrupt *SNAP*. He turned very pale, then spun round and saw that the sea monster was well and truly awake, and looked *very* grumpy to have been disturbed.

'Raise the mainsail!' yelled the captain in alarm. 'Raise the foresail! Raise all the sails and let's go, go, **GO**, me hearties. I don't want to be that monster's lunch!'

'Talking of lunch,' Cannonball said, picking up his cooking pot and eyeing what was left inside. 'Special treat! Does anyone want—'

'No!' Halibut screamed. 'Nobody wants your disgusting stew! Do something useful for once and help us get out of here. **NOW!**'

The pirates ran around frantically, raising the sails and doing what they could to steer the ship away. But the sea monster uncoiled its

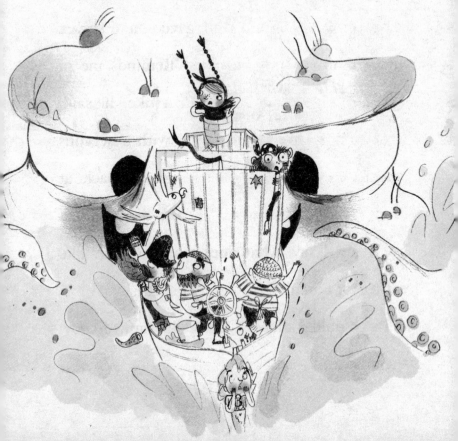

long, thick tail and followed them through the water, its red eyes determined.

'Um, Cutlass, is it me,' Patch asked worriedly as they peeped over the edge of the ship, 'or is the sea monster . . . licking its lips?'

Cutlass nodded and gave a shiver. 'Reminds me of a joke,' he said, with a nervous glance back at the creature. 'I say, I say, I say: what does a sea monster like eating for lunch?'

What does a sea monster like eating for lunch?

Patch pulled a face. 'Do I really want to know the answer?'

74

'Fish and ships,' replied Cutlass unhappily. 'Get it, matey? Fish and – **WHOAAA!**' He let out a frightened squawk and flew up into the air as the sea monster suddenly lunged at the *Golden Earring*, revealing a mouth as big as a train carriage that was full of pointy teeth.

'**Yikes!**' screamed Butch, throwing himself down on the deck in terror.

'Mercy!' wailed Cannonball, hiding his face in his apron.

Even the rats seemed alarmed. 'Back to the nest, lads!' one of them squeaked and they all scampered out of sight at once.

Fish and ships!

With Cutlass's joke still ringing in her ears, Patch spotted Cannonball's dropped stew pot and had a brainwave. 'Lunch – that's it!' she cried.

'What, for us? Are you mad? We're about to be eaten alive and you're thinking about *lunch*?' Monty gibbered.

'Not *my* lunch – the monster's lunch,' Patch replied. 'None of *us* like Cannonball's revolting recipes, but you never know! Maybe a starving sea monster would . . .'

'He certainly looks crazy enough,' Cutlass agreed.

'Come on, let's see if we can tempt it,' Patch said, sprinting across to the stinking stew. 'Monty, help me push this overboard.

Use some of that monkey muscle.'

'**Heave! Heave! Heave!**' Cutlass called as Patch and Monty shoved the heavy stew pot to the side of the ship and hoisted it up.

'Oi!' bellowed Cannonball just then, seeing what they were up to.

But he was too late because in the very next moment . . .

'**Heave ho!**' yelled Patch, and she and Monty gave the stew pot one final push and sent it sailing overboard.

SPLASH!

It landed right in front of the sea monster's nose, splattering it with cold water and hot stew.

'**GRAAAAARRGHHHH!**' roared the monster as the sea salt stung its eyes.

'My new pan!' cried Cannonball in outrage, rushing to the side of the ship.

Down below, the stew pot was bobbing like a tiny boat on the surface of the water. The sea monster gave it a suspicious sniff . . . then opened its enormous red mouth and **gobbled** the stew right up, pot and all.

Gulp! **BUUUURRRRRP!** went the monster, and the *Golden Earring* rocked from side to side with the force of the sound. A seagull dropped from the sky in shock. A dolphin went temporarily deaf. And everyone on board the ship held their breath anxiously as they waited to see what the monster would do next.

Chapter Five

'Am I imagining things,' Cannonball asked wonderingly, 'or is that sea monster . . . sort of . . . *smiling*?'

'Wobbling walruses, I think the man's right for once,' Captain Halibut breathed.

'It's licking its lips!' Cutlass cried, high-fiving Patch claw to paw as the sea monster gazed hopefully at the ship. He laughed. 'For the first time ever, a living creature might just have *enjoyed* one of Cannonball's meals.'

'I can hardly believe my eye,' Patch said, astonished.

Cannonball was looking rather proud of himself. 'Glad you enjoyed it, laddie,' he called to the monster, who swam up to the *Golden Earring* and butted its head against it. As the whole ship shook – *DOINGGGGG* – the monster opened its mouth wide, like a baby bird waiting to be fed.

'It wants more!' Ginger realized.

'It actually *liked* it!' Butch marvelled, pinching his arm in case he was having a very weird dream. '*Ow!*' No, he wasn't having a very weird dream. This was happening, in real life. The sea monster seemed to seriously want second helpings of Cannonball's cooking.

It was a miracle!

'What are you waiting for, you **brainless blaggard**?' the captain yelled at Cannonball as they all stood staring in amazement. 'Arrrr! Go and get the creature something else to eat, on the double!'

Cannonball did not need telling twice. He was delighted to have an eager diner for a change! 'Here you are, me hearty!' he called out, tossing the remains of last night's catfish curry overboard.

SPLISH.

Gulp! went the monster, gobbling it up in one mouthful, plate and all. *BUUURRRP*.

'Squid crumble!' announced Cannonball, lobbing down a bowl of crusty grey gloop.

SPLASH.

Gulp! went the monster, scoffing the lot in one go. ***BUUURRRP***.

'Roast albatross pie!' cried Cannonball, hurling the dish overarm, as if he was playing cricket.

SPLOSH.

Gulp! went the monster, knocking it back immediately. ***BUUURRRP***. Then it looked lovingly up at Cannonball while a strange and disgusting belly rumble made the sea tremble around it.

A nearby pelican fainted and a sea turtle started crying.

'Is there anything else we can give it?' asked Ginger, seeing the monster opening its mouth again.

'Not really,' Cannonball confessed. Then his eye fell upon Patch, Cutlass and Monty, and he scratched his head with a wooden spoon. 'Unless . . .'

'Not likely!' Patch yelped, scampering away at once. 'Over here, guys, before he feeds us to the monster. **Quick!**'

Meanwhile, Captain Halibut was checking his watch. 'Glad as I am that you've found yourself an admirer, Cannonball, we do have a race to win.' He gave the sea monster a stern look. 'So that's your lot, monstrous matey. We've got to find our way to Hammerhead Island.' He rapped his telescope against the side of the ship. 'All hands on deck!' he ordered his crew. 'If I remember the map rightly, we should head full east now. Heave ho!'

'Aye aye, Cap'n,' said Butch, hurrying to take the wheel once more. 'The sooner we get out of this Sea of Really, Really Bad Things, the better!'

'Hmm,' said Patch, watching as the monster nudged impatiently at the ship. *BOOF*. *BASH*. *THUD*. 'I'm not sure Cannonball's lunch guest understood the meaning of "that's your lot", you know. It still looks pretty hungry to me.'

The sea monster did indeed seem annoyed

at having its meal cut short. It flicked its long tail crossly, sending a huge wave splashing onto a small desert island nearby. Its big, blubbery bottom lip stuck out sulkily.

Then it bared its teeth and growled.

'Yikes! Nobody panic, but I think the monster is getting kind of angry,' Butch whimpered, peeping at it from between his fingers.

Suddenly the monster gave a roar, opened its mighty jaws and tried to *bite* the ship. **CHOMP!**

Cannonball yelled in panic.

Butch screamed and had a little accident.

Ginger fell over in fright and went face first into the spilled stew.

'I was only joking about the fish and ships!' squawked Cutlass in alarm, hiding behind a barrel of gunpowder with Monty.

Even Captain Halibut looked worried. 'Blasted barnacles, this is a rum rogue!' he cried, snatching a frying pan from Cannonball's apron pocket and hurling it down at the beast. 'Get out of it, you! Leave my ship alone!'

CLONK! went the pan on the sea monster's head.

'**GRAAAAAARRGH**!' it roared furiously.

'My frying pan!' Cannonball wailed.

'This has gone far enough,' Patch said to her pals. 'We've got to scare the monster away once and for all.' Cutlass and Monty peeped out from behind the barrel at her, and Patch beamed. 'And you've just given me the idea of how to do it!'

'We have?' Cutlass asked in surprise.

Patch let out a blood-freezing *yowl*, so loud that the rest of the crew all turned to stare at her. Then she jumped up onto the nearest cannon and pointed a paw meaningfully at it.

'The cat's trying to tell us something,' Ginger realized. 'What is it, Patch? Have you hurt your paw?'

'She's hungry,' Cannonball guessed.

'She wants her mummy?' Butch whimpered,

knees knocking. '**ME TOO**.'

Patch sighed. These pirates were hopeless! 'If they fire the cannons, they'll scare the monster away,' she told Cutlass and Monty. 'Help me explain!'

Patch walked up and down the cannon while Monty mimed lighting it.
Cutlass even flew over
to the

gunpowder barrel and pecked at it pointedly.

BOOF. ***BASH***. ***THUD***. The monster was still taking its bad mood out on the *Golden Earring*. Patch pointed her paw at the cannon again, desperate for the pirates to understand.

'I've got absolutely no idea what that maggot-brained moggy is doing up there,' Captain Halibut said, 'but, shiver me timbers, I've just had the most excellent idea, crew. Time to show that monster who's boss around here and send it packing. Fire in the hole!'

Patch, Cutlass and Monty only just managed to dodge out of the way before there was a thunderous ***BOOM! BOOM! BOOM!*** and the smell of gunpowder as Captain Halibut fired the ship's cannons one after another.

Flinching in fright, the sea monster backed away hurriedly. And also . . .

'Wait, what's that?' Patch asked, rubbing her eye in disbelief, because there, flying through the air away from the ship were . . .

'Eeek! Squeak! Whee! Whoaaa!'

A shower of *very* surprised-looking rats!

'They must have made their nests in the cannons,' Patch cried, staring wide-eyed as the rats shot across the water and landed – *thumpety thump thump thump* – on the tiny desert island nearby. Double bonus! Then she grinned and waved a paw. 'Goodbyeeee! Don't come back!'

'Whoa, rats are *tough*,' Cutlass said admiringly, as the rats brushed off their fur, licked their sooty tails clean and set about exploring their new island home.

'They're tough – and they're not our problem any more!' Patch said, and high-fived her pals. **'Phew!'**

Even better, the sea monster wasn't their problem any more either. Scared off by the cannons, it circled the desert island – licking its lips as if it loved the smell of the rats even more than it loved the taste of Cannonball's cooking.

'And now for a very swift getaway,' Captain Halibut said, wiping his brow. 'All hands on deck, me hearties! Let's get out of here as fast as we can!'

Chapter Six

The *Golden Earring* pirates sailed speedily away, and Patch hoped that their luck was about to change for the better. And did it?

No! The Sea of Really, Really Bad Things turned out to be a truly *horrible* place. First, the *Golden Earring* sailed past a shipwreck with what looked worryingly like a bunch of *zombie pirates* patrolling up and down the deck. **Yikes!**

Then they met a gang of really scary-looking sharks, one of which seemed to be chewing on an actual pirate *leg* as it swam along beside them. *Eek!*

Worst of all was the cloud of biting insects they sailed through, which nipped and nibbled at the crew as if they were a feast, leaving itchy red lumps all over them.

'**Ow!**'

'**Ooh!**'

'**Argh!**'

'This is the worst shortcut *ever*,' Monty complained, rubbing his back against the mast to scratch it.

'The Sea of Really, Really Bad Things is a complete nightmare,' Patch agreed, trying to shake the horrid insects from her fur.

'I can't wait for this race to be over,' Cutlass

groaned, gazing at his spotty reflection in the shiny ship's bell. 'I hate this horrible sea!'

The pirates, too, were mighty fed up. 'Captain, don't panic, but I think we're actually really totally lost now,' said Butch, staring at the tattered remains of the map. 'And you know me, not scared of anything, but . . . Well, what if we never reach dry land again? We'll all starve, or maybe have to eat each other, and everyone will want to eat *me* first, just because I'm the biggest and that would be so unfair—'

'All right! Yes! I get it!' Captain Halibut grumbled. He was one of those people who hated to admit they might have got something wrong. 'Shiver me timbers, stop blubbering. We're not lost, you **lily-livered lummox**. We're just . . . taking the interesting way there.'

At that moment, they heard a little splash from the sea below – and then up popped a familiar friendly mermaid. '*Cooee!* Anybody need some help? Not lost, are you, by any chance?'

'*Lost?*' blustered Captain Halibut, his moustache bristling indignantly. 'Certainly not! We know perfectly well where we're—'

'We *are* lost, Shelly!' Ginger called down from the lookout. 'We are *so* lost!'

'We don't have a clue where we're going,' Cannonball agreed from where he was swabbing the last stew splashes off the deck.

'And some of the crew – not me – are getting a bit worried that we'll be lost forever,' Butch added. 'And eaten!'

Shelly the mermaid smiled. 'I thought you probably *were* lost,' she replied, 'seeing as you're heading straight for the **Zone of Doom and Disaster**. It's even worse than the Sea of Really, Really Bad Things, you know.

Few pirates ever make it out of there alive!' She turned a somersault and the scales on her tail gleamed greeny-blue in the sunshine.

'Yes, well . . .' coughed Captain Halibut, looking embarrassed. And worried.

'**D-D-Doom** and **D-D-Disaster?**' Butch echoed fearfully, knees knocking together. 'I don't like the sound of **Doom and Disaster**. Not one little tiny bit!'

Patch leaped up onto the ship's railing and waved a paw at the mermaid. 'We want to go to Hammerhead Island,' she mewed down to her. 'Is it far from here?'

The mermaid – who was excellent at speaking cat, as well as all sorts of fishy languages – winked up at Patch then addressed the crew. 'If, by any chance, you pirates are sailing to Hammerhead Island,' she said to them, 'you need to head north-west from here. All the way until you see the lighthouse. The island's just after that. Here, let me set you in the right direction.'

And then, to everyone's astonishment, she grabbed hold of the ship's prow and tugged it round. 'There you are. Byeee!' she called out. And with another flick of her tail, she vanished.

'Shelly is so cool,' sighed Ginger. 'I want to be a mermaid when I grow up.'

'Whoa,' breathed Butch in astonishment. 'How did she know where we wanted to go? It was like she read our minds!'

'Nice one, Cap'n,' said Cutlass as Patch leaped down again with a grin. 'Reminds me of a joke – I say, I say, I say: why did the

mermaid blush?'

'Because she was

embarrassed

Why did the mermaid blush?

about the

brainless

pirates she'd

just met?' Patch guessed with a laugh.

'No – because the sea*weed*,' Cutlass chuckled.

'Get it, matey? The mermaid blushed because

the sea weed!'

'That's *wee-ly* awful,' Patch groaned.

Because the seaweed!

But at least seeing Shelly had put the pirates in a better mood. 'Next stop, Hammerhead Island,' Captain Halibut called out bossily, checking the ship's compass. 'Where we'll be picking up first prize in the Great Pirate Race. Yo-ho-ho!'

Chapter Seven

Before long, the *Golden Earring* and her crew had left the Sea of Really, Really Bad Things far behind them and were sailing into friendlier waters. There were no more sea monsters. No zombie pirates. No bloodthirsty sharks. Just calm blue seas, the occasional smiling dolphin and sunshine sparkling on the water. And then . . .

'Lighthouse ahoy!' called Ginger from up in the lookout, and everyone cheered.

'At last!' cried Patch gladly, stretching her paws.

Cutlass peered beadily at the harbour as they approached. 'Oh dear,' he sighed. 'I hate to say it, but I don't think we've won anything. We're certainly not the first ship to reach Hammerhead Island.'

Captain Halibut, squinting through his telescope, had come to the same conclusion. 'Poop decks,' he grumbled, seeing the cluster of ships already moored in the harbour. 'Suffering sea lions, how did that lot manage to finish the race so quickly? Cheaters, the lot of them, I bet. Never trust a pirate!'

Patch and Cutlass looked at one another in disbelief. 'Says the pirate captain who tried to cheat with his stupid shortcut,' Patch snorted.

The harbour at Hammerhead Island was

extremely full. There was the *Savage Wolf*, with a great big silver flag flying from the main mast, its sailors all clinking bottles of rum and toasting their success.

'Second place, *woo-hoo!*' they cheered.

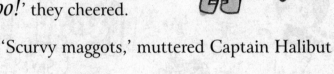

'Scurvy maggots,' muttered Captain Halibut as they sailed past.

Further into the harbour was a ship called *Revenge of the Albatross*, which had an enormous golden flag flying from the main mast. Its sailors were even more cheerful as they danced a pirate reel on deck.

'First prize, *woo-hoo!*' they bellowed.

'Hornswaggling knaves,' growled Captain Halibut as they sailed past.

Further in still, they saw the island's mayor giving the Best-dressed Pirates award to the crew of the *Super Seagull*, who positively gleamed with smartness.

REVENGE OF THE ALBATROSS

Super Seagull

'**Pah!** Call themselves pirates? Perfumed prats, more like,' scowled Captain Halibut as they sailed past.

Butch heaved a heavy sigh. 'We never win anything,' he said, turning away as if he couldn't bear to watch the happy crews celebrate. 'We're rubbish pirates.'

'Hopeless,' Cannonball agreed glumly.

'Still, at least Crunchbone didn't win the race, Cap'n,' Ginger said, clambering down from the crow's nest.

'Is he even here?' asked Cutlass, gazing around.

'Good question,' Patch murmured, scanning the scene. 'Where *is* Captain Crunchbone's snazzy new ship? I can't see it. Can you guys?'

'Nope,' said Monty, dangling from the rigging to get a better view.

'Ha! Let's hope he's lost at sea forever,' Captain Halibut said, looking slightly more cheerful. 'And good riddance too, I say.'

Butch steered the *Golden Earring* into dock. As he did so, Patch couldn't help noticing that several people on the harbourside were pointing at the side of their ship and gasping in surprise. 'What's got them so excited?' she wondered aloud. 'What are they looking at?'

'**Arrrr!** No idea,' Cutlass replied. 'Strange.'

Captain Halibut dropped anchor and Butch leaped ashore to tie up the mooring. By now, a crowd of people had gathered, all gazing at the side of the *Golden Earring* and talking in

113

high-pitched voices. 'Can it be true?' they said.

'Is that what I think it is?'

'Somebody fetch the mayor at once!'

The pirate crew looked at one another in confusion. Then along came the mayor, his huge golden chain glinting as he walked up to the ship.

'*Uh-oh*,' murmured Ginger. 'Do you think we've done something wrong?'

The mayor stopped and stared at the side of the *Golden Earring*. Then he rubbed his eyes and stared again. 'Good gracious,' he said in a faint sort of voice. 'Well, goodness gracious me.' Then he gazed up at Captain Halibut and saluted. 'Most excellent captain, am I to believe my own eyes?' he asked. 'Did you actually encounter the Monster of the Deep . . . and **survive?**'

'The **Monster of the Deep**?' gulped a nearby pirate on the *Howling Curse*.

'Did he really just say "the Monster of the Deep"?' gasped the captain of the *Mighty Man-O'-War*.

'The sea monster? Oh right, yes,' Captain Halibut replied, sounding surprised. 'We gave it some leftovers and fired a load of rats out of the cannons and . . .' He straightened his jacket, suddenly aware that everyone in the harbour was listening. 'And it was a *terrible* fight it put up, Mr Mayor,' he went on in a gruff voice. 'The biggest, most **bloodthirsty** battle in pirating history was had. **Arrrr!**'

Captain Halibut lowered the gangplank and strode down to the dockside, *stamp*-*clonk*,

stamp-*clonk*, followed by the rest of the pirate

crew. Patch blinked as she saw what everyone else

had been pointing at: the huge sharp tooth that

was sticking out of the side of the *Golden Earring*. It must have been wrenched from the monster's mouth when the beast tried to **chomp** its way into the ship. No wonder so many people were staring!

Captain Halibut tossed his black curls proudly and stood a little taller. How he loved this moment of glory! 'Of course, there was *one* member of the crew who was braver than all the rest,' he boasted. 'And that was . . .'

His lips were just forming the word 'me' when Monty trod on Patch's tail.

117

'**MEOW!**' yowled Patch, leaping away . . .

right into the arms of the captain, who was too

startled to finish his sentence.

'The cat? The cat was the bravest member of

the crew?' the mayor said eagerly.

'**Hooray for the cat!**' somebody in

the crowd cheered.

Captain Halibut's face turned beetroot at

their mistake. 'Well, no . . .' he tried to argue,

but it was too late. The whole crowd was smiling and applauding Patch.

'Hooray for the cat! Captain Cat!' they shouted.

Still in the captain's arms, Patch licked a paw modestly. 'Aw, shucks!' She grinned at Cutlass before leaping down and going to rub her head against the mayor's ankles.

'Adorable!' he cooed, reaching down to stroke her. 'Well, Captain Cat, it looks like you'll be having a very fine fish dinner tonight,' he said, straightening up once more, 'because I'm delighted to announce that the *Golden Earring* crew has most definitely won the Bravest Pirates award. Congratulations! Or should I say *con-cat-ulations*?'

'Terrible,' groaned Cutlass, hiding his face in his wing. 'Word of advice, mate: leave the jokes to the parrot.'

After that, things got even better. Everyone wanted to make a fuss of Patch – and a friendly fisherman gave her not one, not two, but *three* yummy fresh mackerel from that day's catch.

'Mmmm, fish . . .' sighed Patch dreamily as she tucked in.

The other crew members were overjoyed too.

'I knew I was brave!' smiled Butch, flexing his muscles as the mayor handed out their medals. 'Arrrr!'

'It's the **best day ever**,' cried Ginger, dancing a jig with Monty. 'Wait till I tell my mum and dad!'

'This calls for my famous prawn-and-pebble pudding for tea tonight,' Cannonball said happily. 'With real pebbles. **Special treat!**'

As for Captain Halibut – his day was well and truly made when a tugboat chugged into the harbour a while later, towing a very sorry-looking ship behind it. Its mast was broken. Its sails were torn. And – oh dear! There was a huge hole in its broadside. 'What the devil . . . ?' murmured Halibut in astonishment.

The mayor turned to see what he was staring at. 'Ahh, yes, very unfortunate,' he said. 'I believe that is Captain Crunchbone's new ship. Word is that the captain . . . er . . . slipped in a pile of . . . well, *monkey sick*, apparently – and then somehow slid all the way over to his cannons and managed to set them off *into* his own ship. Don't ask me how. Poor chap. Not had a good day. I'm told the ship is a total write-off.'

There was a gleam in Captain Halibut's eye, as if he was trying very hard not to smirk. 'Arrrr! A great shame!' he replied unconvincingly. 'Some people are just **not** cut out for the pirating life, are they?'

Patch couldn't help a giggle as she noticed the forlorn-looking figure of Crunchbone in the back of the tugboat. His red hair appeared flattened and frizzy, and he was shivering inside a fluffy yellow blanket. The rest of his crew was huddled together, all looking green-faced as the boat bounced along the water. 'Monkey sick, eh?' she whispered to Monty and Cutlass. 'I wonder how *that* got on his ship?' Her wink was enough to say that *of course* she remembered *exactly* where it had come from!

'Good old Monty,' laughed Cutlass. 'He's a chimp off the old block. Get it, mateys? A *chimp* off the old block!'

As the sun began to go down at the end of that long and eventful day, Patch the pirate cat was feeling very content. So were the rest of the crew!

With their winnings, Captain Halibut had treated himself to a splendid new hat from the posh pirate outfitters in town, and he'd made sure that his crew members had a few gold coins to spend too.

Cannonball had bought himself another shiny

stew pot as well as a brand-new recipe book,
Monstrously Good Meals. He had a feeling that
it might come in handy if they ever
got lost at sea again.

Ginger had spent her money on a new stash

of emergency snacks and a postcard to send to

her mum and dad. She'd also

found some new

sunglasses,

which made her look even more cool than the last pair.

As well as treating the ship to a plastic-covered map that was completely chew-proof, Butch hadn't been able to resist buying a stick of candyfloss as big as his head. He then spent the rest of the day making up a new pirate shanty that he'd been singing ever since.

'Yo-ho-ho, and a crossbones flag,
We're the bravest pirates and won the swag!
"But who's the best one?" I hear you call.
Butch is the answer – the toughest of them all!'

As for Patch, Cutlass and Monty, they had a lovely time too, being showered with treats and goodies from the islanders. All the same, after a while Patch decided it was time to waddle back to the *Golden Earring* to take up her duties guarding the ship. Partly because she didn't want any more unwelcome ratty visitors on board, but also because even the boldest, bravest pirate captain on all seven of the high seas sometimes needed a little cat nap . . .

THE END

THE END

Turn the page for an exclusive extract

from Captain Cat's first adventure . . .

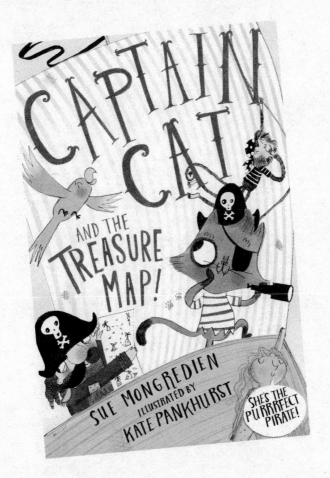

It was a sunny morning on board the *Golden Earring* and Patch the pirate puss was patrolling the ship, sniffing the salty sea air.

There was Cutlass the green pirate parrot, thinking up brilliant new jokes.

There was Monty the annoying ship's monkey, picking his fleas and eating bananas.

And there was Captain Halibut, working hard as usual . . . Oh. Wait, no, he wasn't. He was putting his foot up and snoozing in a deckchair.

Patch gave her claws a sneaky sharpening on

the mast while he wasn't looking.

'Tum-te-tum,' she hummed under her breath.

Around the other side of the ship, a
disgusting stink

wafted out from the galley kitchen where the ship's cook, Cannonball, was making his famous tentacle stew. Famously BAD, that is. Patch hurried quickly through the pong, eyes watering. *Yuck*.

An even more revolting smell wafted out from the ship's toilet where Butch . . . well, actually, let's not go into details about what Butch was doing.

'Pooh,' muttered Patch, wrinkling her nose and walking even faster.

Exactly.

Meanwhile, Ginger was in the crow's nest. She was the only pirate brave enough to climb all the way up there. 'Eleven o'clock and all's well, me hearties,' she called down.

Arrrr, this is the life, thought Patch, settling down in a warm spot of sunshine for a cosy cat-nap. The ship was peaceful. Everything was calm. Shush . . . *shush* . . . sighed the sea against the sides of the ship and, for once, even the screeching seagulls fell silent.

Then the trouble started.

BANG! went the kitchen door, swinging open as Cannonball staggered out. He was carrying an enormous pot, piled so high with potatoes that he couldn't see over the top of them.

'Ginger!' he yelled. 'Where is she? Ginger, I've got a job for you!'

'Ahoy!' Ginger replied cheerfully, scrambling down the rigging. 'On my way, Cannonball.'

Patch opened her one green eye and spied Monty, who was chortling naughtily as he chucked a banana skin in front of the cook.

'Uh-oh!' she cried, jumping up at once. But she was too late.

Cannonball stepped on the banana skin and his feet skidded out from under him. *Wheeeeee!* 'Whoooaaa!' he shouted.

THUMP!

'Oof!' went the cook, landing splat on his back.

CLANG! went the pot as it dropped from his hands.

THUD **THUD** THUD THUD THUDDETY THUD went the potatoes rolling and bowling all over the deck.

As the wave of spuds thundered straight at her,

Patch leapt out the way, her paws outstretched.

'Meooow!' she cried in alarm.

6

'Watch out!' squawked Cutlass.

'Wahhhh!' yelped Ginger, swerving to dodge the flying cat. But she swerved a bit too far, and . . .

SPLOSH! Ginger plunged headfirst into the sea, splattering the snoozing captain with cold, salty water.

'What the . . . ?' spluttered Captain Halibut, falling out of his deckchair.

'HELP!' wailed Ginger from the water, arms flailing.

'PIRATE OVERBOARD!' screeched Cutlass, flying around in circles. 'GINGER OVERBOARD!'

Unfortunately, none of the pirates understood parrot language. They didn't speak cat or monkey either. While this meant that Patch, Cutlass and Monty could say anything they liked about the crew without them knowing, it also meant that sometimes – like now! – it wasn't very easy to alert the pirates to danger.

Hearing the racket, Butch charged out from the toilet, still pulling up his pants.

'NOBODY PANIC!' he bellowed. But then he saw his shipmate struggling in the sea and clapped his hands to his face. 'HELP! SHE'S GOING TO DROWN!' he shrieked.

Cannonball sat up and rubbed his round, shiny head. 'My potatoes . . .' he moaned.

'Devil's dogfish,' growled Captain Halibut, stamping to the side of the ship. *Stamp*-clonk, *stamp*-clonk went the sound of his wooden leg.

'What's all the rumpus?'

'I'm . . . *blub-blub-blub* . . . sinking!' gulped Ginger, thrashing about below.

Honestly, thought Patch, strolling across the deck towards a large coil of rope. *Sometimes pirates are soooo useless!* She shoved at the rope with her paws, sending one end snaking over the side of the ship.

'Ahoy, Cutlass!' she yelled, and the parrot flapped across the ship, grabbed the rope in his beak and swooped down with it to Ginger.

Then he fluttered back to high-five Patch, claw to paw.

Patch smiled. 'Easy-peasy!'

'Heave! Heave! Heave!' grunted Butch, doing his best to haul Ginger out of the sea.

9

'*Coo-ee!* Let me help!' came a voice. Patch peered overboard to see a mermaid who'd just popped up in the sea nearby.

'**Hurrrggh-ha!**' And with her mighty mermaid muscles she gave Ginger a powerful push.

'**Whoaaa!**' yelled Ginger, flying through the air. She fell onto the deck, dripping wet and puffing like a puffer fish. 'Phew. Thanks, Shelly!' she called to the friendly mermaid, who gave her a cheerful wave in return. Then Ginger shook herself dry, sneezed some seaweed out of her nose and held up a green glass bottle with a cork in one end.

'Guys, look what I found,' she said with a watery grin.

'Is it rum?' asked Cannonball hopefully.

Ginger yanked out the cork with her teeth and peered into the bottle.

'There's some paper inside,' she said, pulling it out carefully. 'Ooh!' she exclaimed, dropping the bottle as she unrolled a weathered old scroll. 'It's a map!'

Patch pricked up her ears at Ginger's excited voice. *A map? Cool!*

Ginger peered at the parchment, scratching her head. 'Cuh-cuh-CUSTARD, tuh-tuh-TREATS map!' she spelled out, then beamed. 'Oh yay, I love custard!'

Cutlass landed on a nearby cannon. 'I say, I say, I say: what's yellow and stupid?' he squawked to Patch.

'I know what's *green* and stupid,' called Monty nastily, dangling upside down from the rigging and

Hey, Cap'n, what's yellow and stupid?

showing everyone his horrid pink monkey bottom.

The other two ignored him.

'*Thick* custard,' Cutlass laughed to Patch. 'Get it, matey? **Thick** custard!'

Captain Halibut snatched the map from Ginger.

'I'll have that,' he snapped, then gave one of his legendary nostril-quivering snorts as he read the map. 'It doesn't say *custard treats*, you deep-sea dimwit, it says *cursed treasure*!'

'Talking of thick . . .' Patch whispered to Cutlass.

Thick custard

'Whoops,' said Ginger, looking disappointed. 'I fancied a custard treat.'

Captain Halibut did *not* look disappointed. His moustache was practically waggling with joy. 'Who cares about custard when this is a *treasure* map?' he cheered. 'Goody gumdrops! Butch, steer the ship starboard and bring her about immediately. Keep your eyes peeled for an island. We're going treasure hunting!'

Butch didn't move – apart from his big burly knees, which were knocking together with fright. 'But, C-c-captain . . . what about the c-c-curse?' he said, his voice going wibbly-wobbly. 'C-c-cursed treasure sounds d-d-dangerous.'

'Codswallop,' scoffed the captain. 'If there's

14

treasure for the taking, then I'm the pirate to pilfer it. Hard starboard, I say – and see to it smartly. **Heave ho!**'

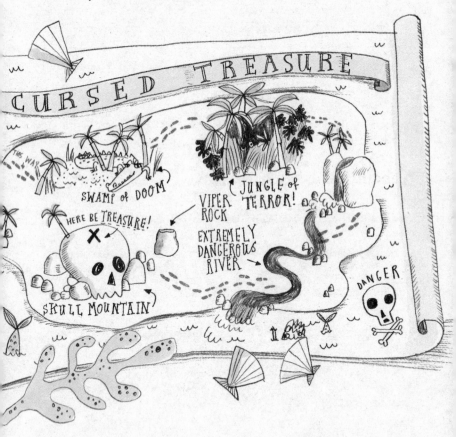

About the author

Sue Mongredien has had over one hundred children's books published, including the Oliver Moon and Secret Mermaid series for Usborne, and the Prince Jake books for Orchard. She is also one of the authors behind the internationally bestselling Rainbow Magic series, as Daisy Meadows. She lives in Bath with her husband and their three children. *Captain Cat and the Great Pirate Race* is the second in the Captain Cat series.

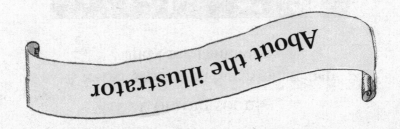

About the illustrator

Kate Pankhurst lives in Leeds with her family and her spotty dog, Olive. She has a studio based in an old spinning mill where she writes and illustrates children's books. Recent projects have included the bestselling Fantastically Great Women series and the Mariella Mystery Investigates series. Kate is distantly related to the suffragette Emmeline Pankhurst, something that has been an influence on the type of books she enjoys creating for children.

THE REAL FAMILY CHRISTMAS
3 FESTIVE STORIES IN 1

Sue Mongredien
ILLUSTRATED BY
Kate Pankhurst

Coming soon!
A festive treat from Sue Mongredien
and Kate Pankhurst.